TOM THUMB
AND
OTHER FAVORITES

THE GROLIER SOCIETY INC. • NEW YORK

Contents

TOM THUMB

With Drawings by
L. Leslie Brooke

TOM THUMB

L ONG ago, in the merry days of good King Arthur, there lived a ploughman and his wife. They were very poor, but would have been contented and happy if only they could have had a little child. One day, having

heard of the great fame of the magician Merlin, who was living at the Court of King Arthur, the wife persuaded her husband to go and tell him of their trouble. Having arrived at the Court, the man besought Merlin with tears in his eyes to give them a child, saying that they would be

quite content even though it should be no bigger than his thumb. Merlin determined to grant the request, and what was the countryman's astonishment to find when he reached home that his wife had a son, who, wonderful to relate, was no bigger than his father's thumb!

The parents were now very happy, and the christening of the little fellow took place with great ceremony. The Fairy Queen, attended by all her company of elves, was present at the feast. She kissed the little child, and, giving it the name of Tom Thumb, told her fairies to fetch the

L.L.B.

tailors of her Court, who dressed her little godson according to her orders. His hat was made of a beautiful oak leaf, his shirt of a fine spider's web, and his hose and doublet were of thistledown, his stockings were made with the rind of a delicate green apple, and the garters were two of the

finest little hairs imaginable, plucked from his mother's eyebrows, while his shoes were made of the skin of a little mouse. When he was thus dressed, the Fairy Queen kissed him once more, and, wishing him all good luck, flew off with the fairies to her Court.

As Tom grew older, he became very amusing and full of tricks, so that his mother was afraid to let him out of her sight. One day, while she was making a batter pudding, Tom stood on the edge of the bowl, with a lighted candle in his hand, so that she might see that the pudding was made properly. Unfortunately, however, when her back was turned, Tom fell into the bowl, and his

mother, not missing him, stirred him up in the pudding, tied it in a cloth, and put it into the pot. The batter filled Tom's mouth, and prevented him from calling out, but he had no sooner felt the hot water, than he kicked and struggled so much that the pudding jumped about in the pot, and his mother, thinking the pudding was bewitched, was nearly frightened out of her wits. Pulling it out of the pot, she ran with it to her door, and gave it to a tinker who was passing. He was very thankful for it, and looked forward to having a better dinner than he had enjoyed for many a long day. But his pleasure did not last long, for, as he was getting over a stile, he happened

to sneeze very hard, and Tom, who had been quite quiet
inside the pudding for some time, called out at the top of
his little voice, "Hallo, Pickens!" This so terrified the

tinker that he flung away the pudding, and ran off as fast
as he could. The pudding was all broken to pieces by
the fall, and Tom crept out, covered with batter, and ran

home to his mother, who had been looking everywhere for
him, and was delighted to see him again. She gave him a
bath in a cup, which soon washed off all the pudding, and
he was none the worse for his adventure.

A few days after this, Tom accompanied his mother
when she went into the fields to milk the cows, and, fearing
he might be blown away by the wind, she tied him to
a sow-thistle with a little piece of thread. While she was
milking, a cow came by, bit off the thistle, and swallowed
up Tom. Poor Tom did not like her big teeth, and called
out loudly, "Mother, mother!" "But where are you,

Tommy, my dear Tommy?" cried out his mother, wringing her hands. "Here, mother," he shouted, "inside the red cow's mouth!" And, saying that, he began to kick and scratch till the poor cow was nearly mad, and at length

tumbled him out of her mouth. On seeing this, his mother rushed to him, caught him in her arms, and carried him safely home.

Some days after this, his father took him to the fields a-ploughing, and gave him a whip, made of a barley straw, with which to drive the oxen; but little Tom was soon lost in a furrow. An eagle seeing him, picked him up and

flew with him to the top of a hill where stood a giant's castle. The giant put him at once into his mouth, intending to swallow him up, but Tom made such a great disturbance when he got inside that the monster was soon glad to get

rid of him, and threw him far away into the sea. But he was not drowned, for he had scarcely touched the water before he was swallowed by a large fish, which was shortly

afterwards captured and brought to King Arthur, as a present, by the fisherman. When the fish was opened, everyone was astonished at finding Tom inside. He was

at once carried to the King, who made him his Court dwarf.

> Long time he lived in jollity,
>   Beloved of the Court,
> And none like Tom was so esteemed
>   Amongst the better sort.

The Queen was delighted with the little boy, and made him dance a gaillard on her left hand. He danced so well that King Arthur gave him a ring, which he wore round his waist like a girdle.

Tom soon began to long to see his parents again, and begged the King to allow him to go home for a short time. This was readily permitted, and the King told him he might take with him as much money as he could carry.

And so away goes lusty Tom,
   With three pence at his back—
A heavy burthen which did make
   His very bones to crack.

He had to rest more than a hundred times by the

way, but, after two days and two nights, he reached his father's house in safety. His mother saw him coming, and ran out to meet him, and there was great rejoicing at his arrival. He spent three happy days at home, and then set out for the Court once more.

Shortly after his return, he one day displeased the King, so, fearing the royal anger, he crept into an empty flower-pot, where he lay for a long time. At last he ventured to peep out, and, seeing a fine large butterfly on the ground close by, he stole out of his hiding-place, jumped on its back, and was carried up into the air. The King and

nobles all strove to catch him, but at last poor Tom fell from his seat into a watering-pot, in which he was almost

drowned, only luckily the gardener's child saw him, and pulled him out. The King was so pleased to have him safe once more that he forgot to scold him, and made much of him instead.

Tom afterwards lived many years at Court, one of the best beloved of King Arthur's knights.

> Thus he at tilt and tournament
>   Was entertained so,
> That all the rest of Arthur's knights
>   Did him much pleasure show.
> With good Sir Launcelot du Lake,
>   Sir Tristram and Sir Guy,
> Yet none compared to brave Tom Thumb
>   In acts of chivalry.

THE THREE BEARS

WITH DRAWINGS BY
L. LESLIE BROOKE

THYME IS HONEY
SAVE IT

THE STORY OF
THE THREE BEARS

ONCE upon a time there were Three Bears, who lived together in a house of their own, in a wood. One of them was a Little, Small, Wee Bear; and one was a Middle-sized Bear, and the other was a Great, Huge Bear. They had each a pot for their porridge; a little pot for the Little, Small, Wee Bear; and a middle-sized pot for the Middle Bear, and a great pot for the Great, Huge

Bear. And they had each a chair to sit in; a little chair
for the Little, Small, Wee Bear; and a middle-sized chair
for the Middle Bear, and a great chair for the Great,

Huge Bear. And they had each a bed to sleep in; a little bed for the Little, Small, Wee Bear; and a middle-sized bed for the Middle Bear, and a great bed for the Great, Huge Bear.

One day, after they had made the porridge for their breakfast, and poured it into their porridge-pots, they walked out into the wood while the porridge was cooling, that they might not burn their mouths by beginning too

soon to eat it. And while they were walking, a little Girl
called Goldenlocks came to the house. First she looked in
at the window, and then she peeped in at the keyhole;
and seeing nobody in the house, she turned the handle of

the door. The door was not fastened, because the Bears were good Bears, who did nobody any harm, and never suspected that anybody would harm them. So Goldenlocks opened the door, and went in; and well pleased she was

when she saw the porridge on the table. If she had been a thoughtful little Girl, she would have waited till the Bears came home, and then, perhaps, they would have asked her to breakfast; for they were good Bears—a little

rough or so, as the manner of Bears is, but for all that very good-natured and hospitable. But the porridge looked tempting, and she set about helping herself.

So first she tasted the porridge of the Great, Huge Bear, and that was too hot for her. And then she tasted the porridge of the Middle Bear, and that was too cold for her. And then she went to the porridge of the Little, Small, Wee Bear, and tasted that; and that was neither too hot nor too cold, but just right, and she liked it so well that she ate it all up.

Then Goldenlocks sat down in the chair of the Great, Huge Bear, and that was too hard for her. And then she sat down in the chair of the Middle Bear, and that was too soft for her. And then she sat down in the chair of the Little, Small, Wee Bear, and that was neither too hard nor too soft, but just right. So she seated herself in it, and there she sat till the bottom of the chair came out, and down she came plump upon the ground.

Then Goldenlocks went upstairs into the bed-chamber in which the three Bears slept. And first she lay down upon the bed of the Great, Huge Bear, but that was too high at the head for her. And next she lay down upon the bed of the Middle Bear, and that was too high at the foot for her. And then she lay down upon the bed of the Little, Small, Wee Bear; and that was neither too high at

the head nor at the foot, but just right. So she covered
herself up comfortably, and lay there till she fell fast asleep.

By this time the Three Bears thought their porridge
would be cool enough; so they came home to breakfast.
Now Goldenlocks had left the spoon of the Great, Huge
Bear standing in his porridge.

"SOMEBODY HAS BEEN AT MY PORRIDGE!"
said the Great, Huge Bear, in his great, rough, gruff voice.

And when the Middle Bear looked at hers, she saw that the spoon was standing in it too.

"SOMEBODY HAS BEEN AT MY PORRIDGE!" said the Middle Bear, in her middle voice. Then the

Little, Small, Wee Bear looked at his, and there was the spoon in the porridge-pot, but the porridge was all gone.

"SOMEBODY HAS BEEN AT MY PORRIDGE, AND HAS EATEN IT ALL UP!" said the Little, Small, Wee Bear, in his little, small, wee voice.

Upon this the Three Bears, seeing that someone had entered their house, and eaten up the Little, Small, Wee Bear's breakfast, began to look about them. Now Goldenlocks had not put the hard cushion straight when she rose from the chair of the Great, Huge Bear.

"SOMEBODY HAS BEEN SITTING IN MY CHAIR!" said the Great, Huge Bear, in his great, rough, gruff voice.

And Goldenlocks had squatted down the soft cushion of the Middle Bear.

"SOMEBODY HAS BEEN SITTING IN MY CHAIR!" said the Middle Bear, in her middle voice.

And you know what Goldenlocks had done to the third chair.

"SOMEBODY HAS BEEN SITTING IN MY CHAIR, AND HAS SAT THE BOTTOM OUT OF IT!" said the Little, Small, Wee Bear, in his little, small, wee voice.

Then The Three Bears thought it necessary that they should make farther search; so they went upstairs into their bedchamber. Now Goldenlocks had pulled the pillow of the Great, Huge Bear out of its place.

"SOMEBODY HAS BEEN LYING IN MY BED!" said the Great, Huge Bear, in his great, rough, gruff voice.

And Goldenlocks had pulled the bolster of the Middle Bear out of its place.

"SOMEBODY HAS BEEN LYING IN MY BED!"
said the Middle Bear, in her middle voice.

And when the Little, Small, Wee Bear came to look at his bed, there was the bolster in its place; and the pillow in its place upon the bolster; and upon the pillow was the head of Goldenlocks — which was not in its place, for she had no business there.

"SOMEBODY HAS BEEN LYING IN MY BED—AND HERE SHE IS!"
said the Little, Small, Wee Bear, in his little, small, wee voice.

Goldenlocks had heard in her sleep the great, rough, gruff voice of the Great, Huge Bear, and the middle

voice of the Middle Bear, but it was only as if she had heard someone speaking in a dream. But when she heard

the little, small, wee voice of the Little, Small, Wee Bear, it was so sharp, and so shrill, that it awakened her at once. Up she started; and when she saw the Three Bears on one side of the bed she tumbled herself out at the other, and ran to the window. Now the window was open, because the Bears, like good, tidy Bears, as they were, always opened their bedchamber window when they got up in the morning. Out Goldenlocks jumped, and ran away as fast as she could run — never looking behind her; and what happened to her afterwards I cannot tell. But the Three Bears never saw anything more of her.

LLB.

FIDDLE-DE-DEE, fiddle-de-dee,
    The fly shall marry the humble-bee.
They went to the church, and married was she:
The fly has married the humble-bee.

MISTRESS MARY, quite contrary,
How does your garden grow?
With cockle-shells, and silver bells,
And pretty maids all a row.

THE lion and the unicorn
    Were fighting for the crown;
The lion beat the unicorn
    All round about the town.

Some gave them white bread,
    And some gave them brown;
Some gave them plum-cake,
    And sent them out of town.

THERE was a crooked man, and he went a
crooked mile;
He found a crooked sixpence against a crooked stile:
He bought a crooked cat, which caught a crooked
mouse,
And they all lived together in a little crooked house.

LITTLE Tommy Tittlemouse
Lived in a little house;
He caught fishes
In other men's ditches.

I HAD a little hen, the prettiest ever seen;
    She washed me the dishes, and kept the house
    clean;
She went to the mill to fetch me some flour;
She brought it home in less than an hour;
She baked me my bread, she brewed me my ale;
She sat by the fire, and told many a fine tale.

JACK SPRAT could eat no fat;
His wife could eat no lean:
And so, betwixt them both, you see
They licked the platter clean.

I F all the world was apple-pie,
And all the sea was ink,
And all the trees were bread and cheese,
    What should we have for drink?

THE man in the wilderness asked me
How many strawberries grew in the sea.
I answered him as I thought good,
As many red herrings grew in the wood.

PUSSY-CAT, pussy-cat, where have you been?
   I've been up to London to look at the queen.
Pussy-cat, pussy-cat, what did you there?
I frightened a little mouse under the chair.

DEEDLE, deedle, dumpling, my son John
Went to bed with his trousers on;
One shoe off, the other shoe on,
Deedle, Deedle, dumpling, my son John.